Topic: Interpersonal Skills   **Subt

Notes to Parents and Teachers:

As a child becomes more familiar reading books, it is important for them to rely on and use reading strategies more independently to help figure out words they do not know.

REMEMBER: PRAISE IS A GREAT MOTIVATOR!

Here are some praise points for beginning readers:

• I saw you get your mouth ready to say the first letter of that word.

• I like the way you used the picture to help you figure out that word.

• I noticed that you saw some sight words you knew how to read!

Book Ends for the Reader!

Here are some reminders before reading the text:

• Point to each word you read to make it match what you say.

• Use the picture for help.

• Look at and say the first letter sound of the word.

• Look for sight words that you know how to read in the story.

• Think about the story to see what word might make sense.

Words to Know Before You Read

alone

first

friends

ignore

popped

recess

sad

yelled

ROSIE ROSS, RECESS BOSS

A Story About Problem Solving

By
Darleen Bailey Beard
Illustrated By
Gisela Bohórquez

Rourke
Educational Media
rourkeeducationalmedia.com

A Division of
Carson Dellosa Education®

Lily loved recess.

4

Then along came Rosie Ross,
Recess Boss.

"Me first!"

"Time's up!"

9

"Rosie Ross," Lily yelled.
"You are TOO bossy!"

"Am not!"

11

"Are too!" Lily said. "And I am going to IGNORE you!"

12

"Then I will ignore you too!" Rosie said.

Lily felt sad. Then she noticed something.

Rosie was always alone.
Was she *lonely*?

Ping!
An idea popped into Lily's head.

"To be friends."

19

Now Lily loves recess ...

with Rosie Ross, Recess Friend!

Book Ends for the Reader

I know...

1. What did Rosie do that upset Lily?
2. Did Rosie think she was being bossy?
3. What did Lily notice about Rosie?

I think...

1. How do you think it made Rosie feel when Lily said she was going to ignore her?
2. Did Lily make a good choice when she asked Rosie to be her friend?
3. What are some other ways Lily could have handled Rosie's bossy behavior?

Book Ends for the Reader

What happened in this book?

Look at each picture and talk about what happened in the story.

About the Author

Darleen Bailey Beard is an award-winning children's book author in Norman, Oklahoma. She lives with her husband, daughter, and granddaughter. Unlike Rosie, Darleen is NOT bossy... well, maybe just a little! Learn more about her at: darleenbaileybeard.com

About the Illustrator

Gisela Bohórquez was born and raised in Bogotá, Colombia. As a child, she was always surrounded by amazing books. She loves to put her whole heart into her work.

Library of Congress PCN Data

Rosie Ross, Recess Boss (A Story About Problem Solving) / Darleen Bailey Beard
(Playing and Learning Together)
ISBN 978-1-73160-589-4 (hard cover)(alk. paper)
ISBN 978-1-73160-425-5 (soft cover)
ISBN 978-1-73160-642-6 (e-Book)
ISBN 978-1-73160-662-4 (ePub)
Library of Congress Control Number: 2018967559

Rourke Educational Media
Printed in the United States of America,
North Mankato, Minnesota

www.rourkeeducationalmedia.com

Edited by: Kim Thompson
Layout by: Kathy Walsh
Cover and interior illustrations by: Gisela Bohórquez